A JESTER & PHARLEY PRODUCT and The JESTER Co., Inc. are trademarks of The Jester Co., Inc.

P.O. Box 817 • Malaga Cove Plaza • Palos Verdes Estates, CA 90274

(310) 544-4733 or toll-free (800) 9-JESTER • Fax: (310) 377-7935

Requests for permission to reproduce any part of this book should be directed to The Jester Co., Inc. • P.O. Box 817 • Malaga Cove Plaza • Palos Verdes Estates, CA 90274

Copies of this book are available in better bookstores or may be ordered from the publisher by sending $20 plus $5 for shipping and handling.

Publisher's Publication Data
Saltzman, David, 1967–1990
The Jester Has Lost His Jingle written and illustrated by David Saltzman, 1st ed.
With an Afterword by Maurice Sendak
p. cm.

Summary: A jester and his helpmate wake up to a world without laughter and set out on a quest to find it.

ISBN 0-9644563-0-3

1. Fools and jesters — Juvenile literature 2. Laughter — Fiction 3. Laughter — Therapeutic use
4. Life Skills — Juvenile literature 5. Rhyme 6. Quests in literature

Library of Congress Catalog Card Number: 95-94179

Design Consultation and Production Coordination: Eileen Delson

Printed in Hong Kong by Kay Lau & Associates

First Edition   10 9 8 7 6 5 4

The Jester Has Lost His Jingle

By David Saltzman

Our story begins quite removed
in a castle far away.
Our story unfolds, unfortunately,
on a very unfortunate day.

You see, this morning when the world awoke,
no one was in any mood to joke.

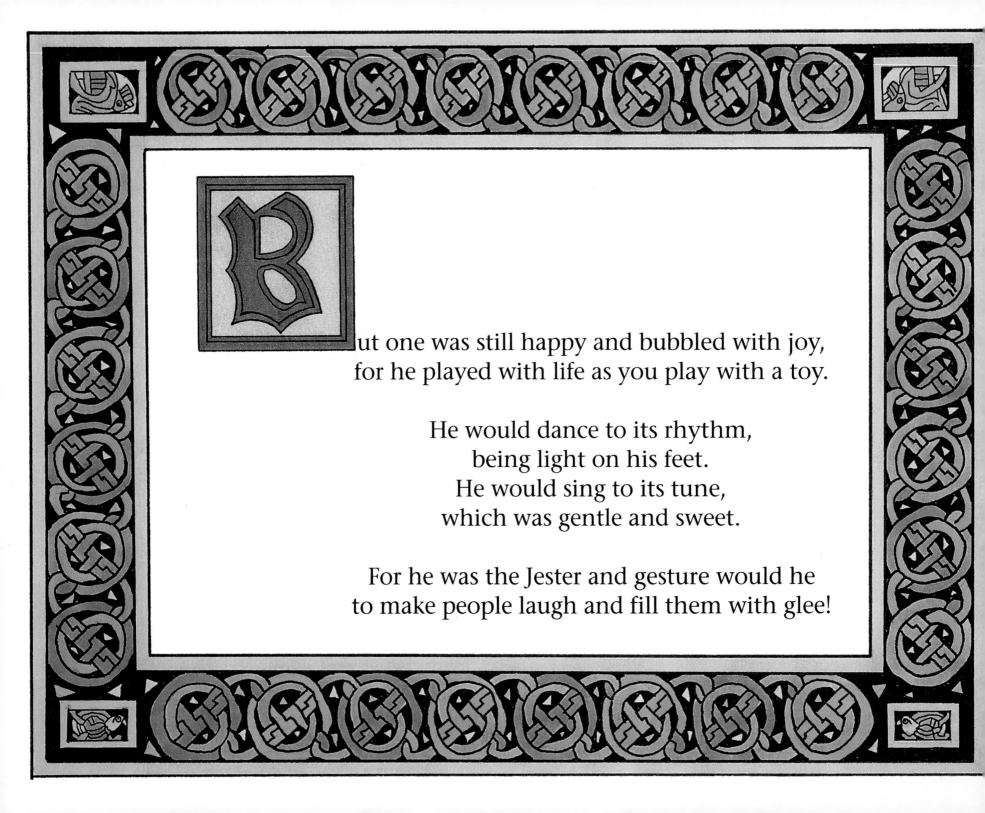

But one was still happy and bubbled with joy,
for he played with life as you play with a toy.

He would dance to its rhythm,
being light on his feet.
He would sing to its tune,
which was gentle and sweet.

For he was the Jester and gesture would he
to make people laugh and fill them with glee!

He had a special helper,
as any jester should.
A friend by name of Pharley,
a piece of talking wood.

He carried Pharley all over.
The two were quite a pair.
They viewed life as a carnival,
a fun-filled, festive fair.

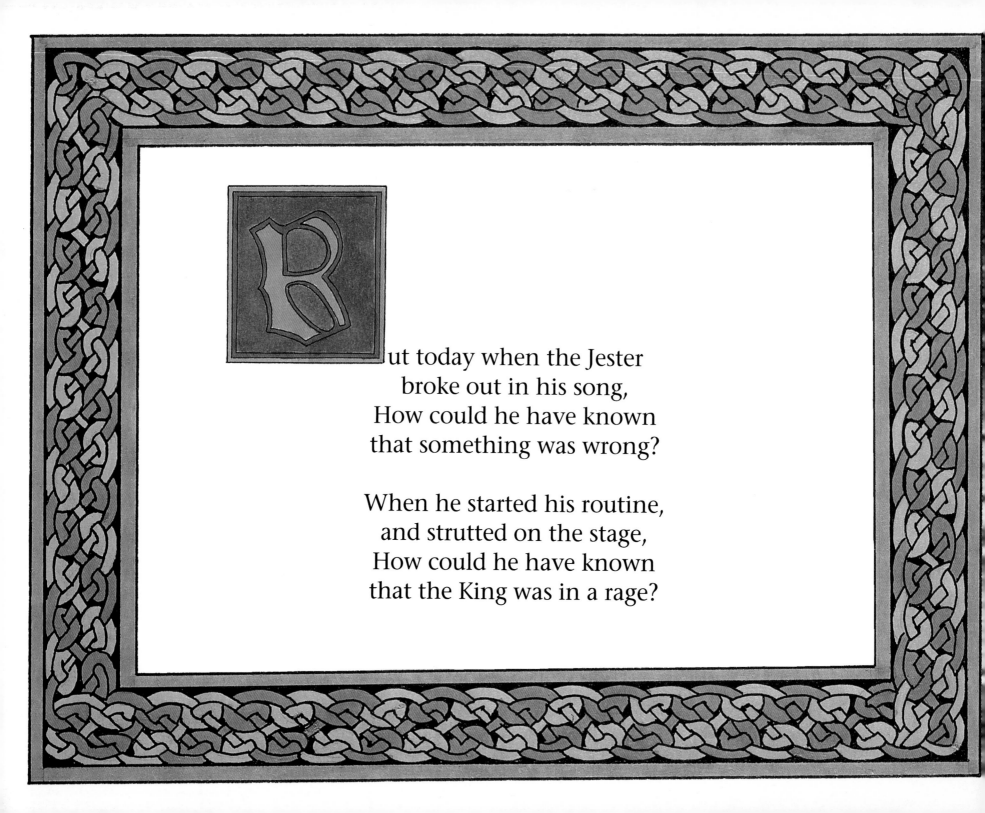

But today when the Jester
broke out in his song,
How could he have known
that something was wrong?

When he started his routine,
and strutted on the stage,
How could he have known
that the King was in a rage?

But nobody giggled.
Nobody yuckled.
Nobody laughed.
And nobody chuckled.

But the King gave no answer. He said nothing more,
merely pointed his finger toward the front door.

The Jester walked out slowly, and a tear fell from his face,
for he'd never left the kingdom, never wandered from this place.

And once outside, the Jester cried,
"Oh Pharley, I fear
what they say is quite true.
I am no longer funny.
My career is quite through."

"That's nonsense!" claimed Pharley.
"You're still funny, I say.
You were funny last week.
You're still funny today!

It seems a nasty rumor,
but laughter must be dead.
The world has lost its sense of humor,"
Pharley sadly said.

"Then it isn't me at all!
It's the world that must be sick.
We must find that sense of humor,
and bring it back here quick!"

So off they went, our fearless two,
to bring back laughter, back to you.

near.

They looked far and near.

They looked far and wide.
They looked everywhere that laughter might hide.

They searched in every corner, under rocks and up in trees.
They peered into the heavens and gazed deep beneath the seas.

They wandered through the country,
through meadows lush and pretty.

They came upon a gleaming bridge that led into a city.

They looked in vain for flowers.
They heard no songs of birds.

But saw lots of angry faces
and heard lots of bitter words.

"Everyone here is so moody.
Everyone here is so mean.

I must confess this city
is the saddest place I've ever seen.

Maybe someone here can tell me.
Maybe someone here might know.

How come people aren't laughing?
How come spirits are so low?"

"Ask that man," Pharley motioned, "that man over there,
the thin one in the alley with the tangles in his hair."
"Okay," said the Jester, "I'll give it a go...
Why are you not laughing sir? I'd really like to know."

"It's kind of hard to laugh or joke
when you're unemployed and completely broke.
I have no job. I have no money.
So tell me, Jester, what's so funny?"

"Oh Pharley, I fear, it's much worse than I thought.
Is laughter something these people forgot?"

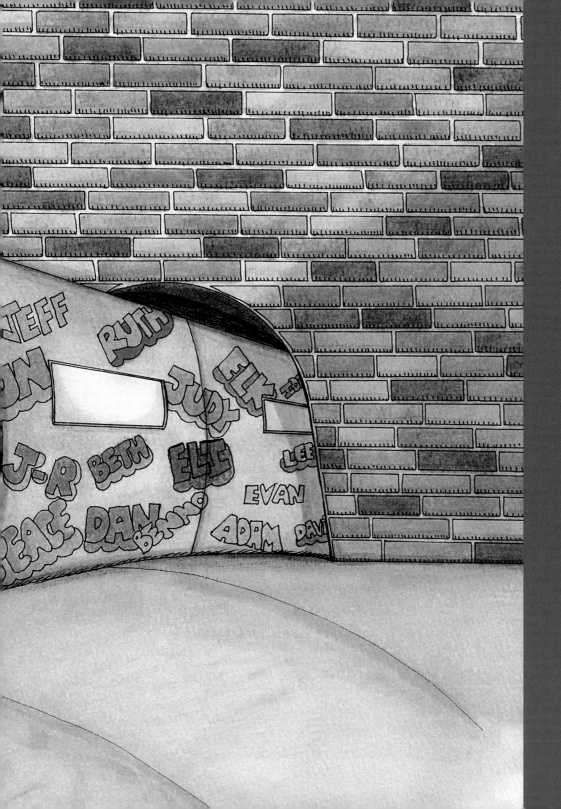

"Impossible!" cried Pharley.
"Why, that's news
I couldn't bear.
Ask that man with
the briefcase,
blowing smoke
into the air."

"Okay," said the Jester,
"I'll try another try...
It seems you don't
believe in laughing, sir.
Can you please
tell me why?"

augh! HA! That's a laugh! The best I've had in years!
The world is not a funny place. It's filled with pain and tears.

Don't you read the papers? It's all there in black and white.

Everything is going wrong, and jokes won't make it right.

I have no time for laughter. I have no time for you.
I'm sorry that's the way things are...

There's nothing YOU can do!"

"Don't believe him," Pharley said. "We know he must be wrong.
Our search for laughter must continue. Time to move along."

The Jester looked up to the sky as he let out a woeful sigh.
He fought back tears and shook his head, then with determination said,

"There must be someone somewhere with a smile upon their face.
There must be someone cheerful in this cold and lonely place.

Say, look at that tall building...perhaps we'll find the answer there.
It's up to us to make a difference. It's up to us to care."

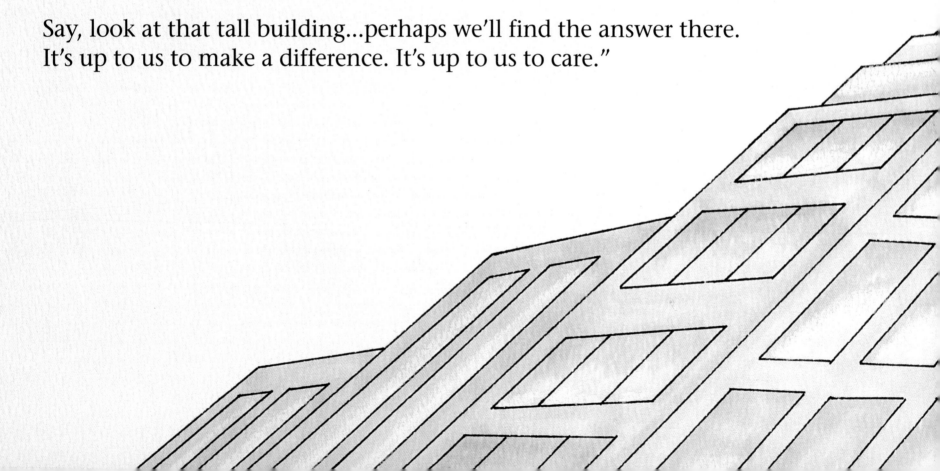

"What of her?" asked Pharley.
"That little girl in bed?

The one who looks so fragile
with the bandage on her head?"

"Hello, little girl," the Jester said.
"My! How do you do?

I wonder if you can tell me,
how come laughter's not with you?"

The little girl looked up and her eyes were opened wide.
She turned slowly to the Jester, and she quietly replied.

"Here I lie, I have a tumor...
And you ask me where's my sense of humor?

I've been very sick.
I'm so tired of trying.

I don't feel like laughing.
I just feel like crying."

"Sometimes I feel like crying too,"
the Jester whispered in her ear.
"But instead of letting teardrops fall,
I make them disappear.

Whenever I feel like crying,
I smile hard instead!
I turn my sadness upside down
and stand it on its head!

When I get sad or lonesome,
or when I get depressed,
that's when I sing my loudest
and dance my very best!"

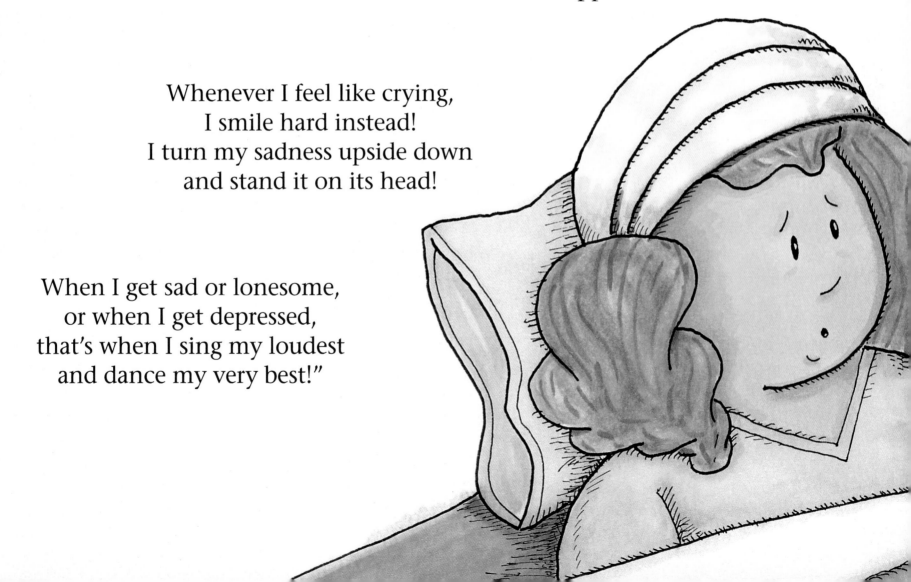

"So won't you try it, little girl?
Won't you laugh with me?
We'll start off very slowly
with a tiny Tee-Hee-Hee."

So he sang his funny song

and he walked his funny walk

and he talked his funny talk.

and he danced his funny dance

And from the room, there came a giggle, which echoed down the halls.
And soon there came another,
which bounced up and down the walls.

The giggle became a snicker,
which grew into a guffaw,
which soon became a chuckle that transformed into a HA!

The Jester was beside himself. He grinned a great big grin.

He hugged and thanked the little girl, and kissed her on the chin.

Soon laughter leaped right out the window,
   growing louder as it flew.

Can't you hear it coming?
It's about to swallow you.

It spread to every corner.
It filled up every space.

Smiles popped up everywhere!
Can't you feel one on your face?

As the Jester ran back to the kingdom,

he carried rainbows in his hand.

And as people started laughing,

colors spread across the land.

He leaped into the palace and he hugged the King and Queen.
He said, "Oh, my high Highness, you won't believe what we have seen!

Laughter isn't missing! Why, it isn't even dead!
Pharley and I have found it!" the Jester proudly said.

"We've found where it's been hiding.
We've discovered where it's been.
It's hiding inside everyone!
It's buried deep within!

Laughter's like a seedling,
waiting patiently to sprout.
All it takes is just a push
to make it pop right out."

"Don't keep it imprisoned
or locked out of sight!
Quickly release it!
It won't hurt or bite!"

So the King said,
"I'll try it...I'll give it a go."
And, all of a sudden, out popped a "HO!"
"That's it!" yelled the Jester.
"Just let it flow!"

And it flowed.

And it flowed.

And it flowed.

nd soon EVERYBODY started giggling!
EVERYBODY started yuckling!
EVERYBODY started laughing!
And EVERYBODY started chuckling!

"My Jester, you have done it," said the King. "You've saved the day!
You've brought back love and laughter and helped us find the way!"

And
when the Jester
heard these words,
he smiled and started singing.
He somersaulted in the air,
for his bells again were ringing!

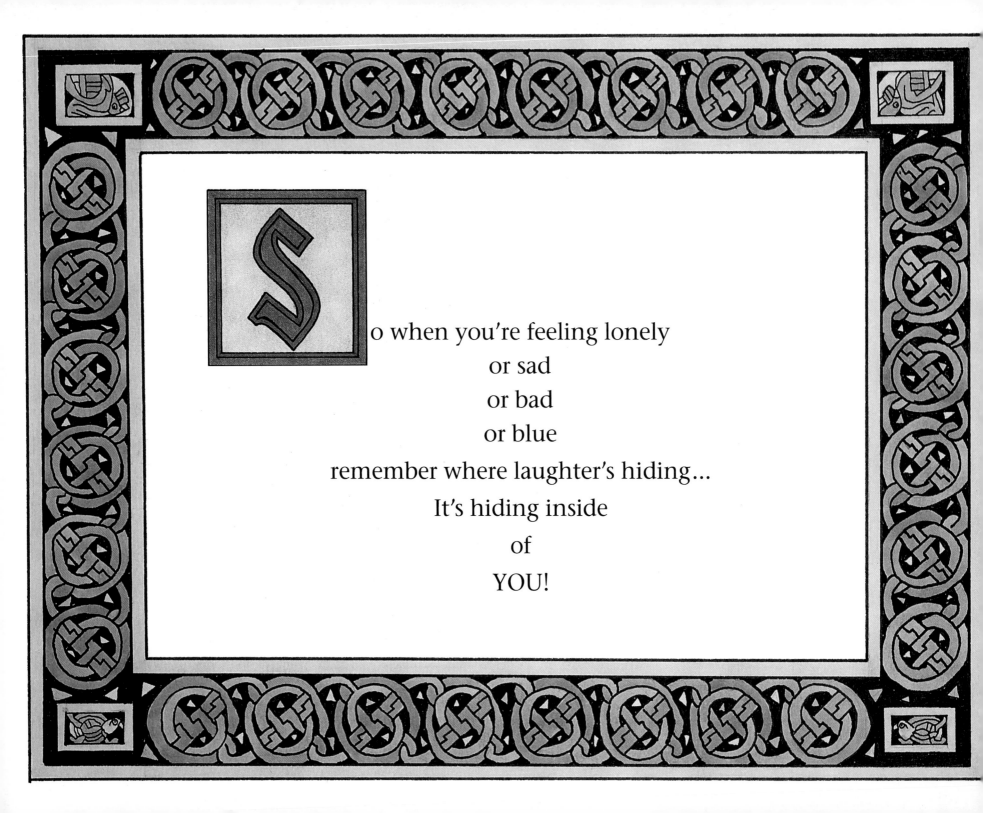

S o when you're feeling lonely
or sad
or bad
or blue
remember where laughter's hiding...
It's hiding inside
of
YOU!

Author's Note

One day during the summer, I walked into the classroom in a very good mood. I was very happy, whistling as I walked. When I arrived into class, I made a silly joke. And nobody laughed. Everybody else was in a horrible mood, caught up in their own lives, their own work, their own problems.

Now I knew that the joke was not very funny, but nobody even smiled or said hello. They just kept to themselves and looked down at the table. My good mood soon became one of depression, rejection and disappointment. I decided to sit silently like the others, thinking to myself how quickly moods change.

I started drawing and, as usual, did not know what I was creating, letting my hand create on its own accord. It turned out to be a very sad-looking face, humped over, trying hard to carry its own weight. I randomly added triangles to his head and, after staring at what I had just made, realized that it looked like a little jester. I added the words next to it: "The jester has lost his jingle."

And thus, the Jester was born.

It is rare for a character of your own creation to come to your aid. Yet, my Jester did just that. During the fall of my senior year at Yale, I was diagnosed as having Hodgkin's disease, a cancer of the lymphatic system. Upon hearing the news, I went out to a patch of lawn, sat by a tree, and cried.

As I sat there crying, I listened to my sobs, thinking how much they sounded like my laughs. And suddenly, one of the lines I had written during the previous summer popped into my head: "Here I lie, I have a tumor...And you ask me where's my sense of humor?" And that was when my Jester came to me. He literally walked over to me, put his hand on my shoulder and with a concerned look said: "David, how come you're not laughing? Your cries sound just like laughs, so why not laugh instead of cry?" I thought about it for a second and then repeated the question to myself: "How come I'm not laughing?"

So I got up from the pile of dead leaves that surrounded me, wiped my face dry of its tears, and walked off laughing at how silly and scary and wonderful this world of ours is.

He came to help me in my time of need, and my hope is that, if you let him, he will come alive within these pages and help you too.

DAVID SALTZMAN

March, 1989

About the Author-Artist

David Saltzman graduated magna cum laude as an English and art major from Yale University in 1989, receiving the David Everett Chantler Award as "the senior who throughout his college career best exemplified the qualities of courage and strength of character and high moral purpose."

Before attending Yale, David went to Chadwick School in Palos Verdes Peninsula in California. It was there that he began his career as a cartoonist with a comic strip called "The Chadwick Chronicles" in which he regularly parodied student life for the school newspaper. He also drew editorial cartoons on local, national and international issues for a Los Angeles Times publication distributed to Southern California high schools.

At Yale, he adapted his character "Pops" into a weekly cartoon strip that chronicled the life of a fictitious Yale professor. He also spun off "Pops" into a series of Yale Academic Calendars and drew weekly editorial cartoons for the Yale Daily News and the Yale Herald.

During his senior year at Yale, David was diagnosed with Hodgkin's disease. For the next year-and-a-half, he kept a comprehensive journal of his thoughts and drawings while completing *The Jester Has Lost His Jingle* and other stories.

In his journal, David wrote, "The best we can do is live life, enjoy it and know it is meant to be enjoyed—know how important and special every time...moment...person is. And at the end of the day say, 'I have enjoyed it, I have really lived the moment.' That is all. All is that. Is. Is is such a powerful word. It's not was or will be. It is IS: Is is alive."

David died on March 2, 1990, 11 days before his 23rd birthday.

Afterword

Our lives briefly touched. But I remember him among all the eager, talented young people I've bumped into along the way. I remember the face—the enthusiasm—the intelligence and unaffected extraordinariness of David Saltzman. It is difficult to remember all the bright, promising youngsters. It is easy to remember David.

That he died before his 23rd birthday is a tragedy beyond words. That he managed through his harrowing ordeal to produce a picture book so brimming with promise and strength, so full of high spirits, sheer courage and humor is nothing short of a miracle. Even the rough patches that David the artist would surely have set to right had he been given the time become all the more precious for the wild light they shed on his urgent, exploding talent.

David was a natural craftsman and storyteller. His passionate picture book is issued out of a passionate heart.

David's Jester soars with life.

—Maurice Sendak
Author-Artist, *Where the Wild Things Are*